SWEET RIDE

a Playing for Keeps novella

CATHRYN FOX

Entangled Publishing, LLC
2614 South Timberline Road
Suite 109
Fort Collins, CO 80525
Visit our website at www.entangledpublishing.com.

Brazen is an imprint of Entangled Publishing, LLC. For more information on our titles, visit www.brazenbooks.com.

Edited by Candace Havens
Cover design by Heather Howland
Cover art from iStock

Manufactured in the United States of America

First Edition November 2015

ENTANGLED
BRAZEN

To Danita, PA extraordinaire. I'd be lost without you.

Chapter One

Alix Harris walked the length of the barn, yelping when a blade of straw cut into the soft flesh between her sandaled toes. Rivulets of perspiration trickled down her cleavage in the stifling heat, plastering the bodice of her dress to her skin. God, she was so not in the mood for this today. She plucked at the expensive fabric, the slight stirring of air doing little to cool her overheated flesh or lighten her mood.

Hot, sweaty, and hardly dressed for a working dude ranch, she haphazardly tucked a long strand of hair back into her once-perfectly-coiffed ponytail. She shook her head, her thoughts rewinding back to a week ago, to when she'd received a hand-delivered invitation promising her a week of R&R at a ranch in cowboy country. She'd had no intention of going until—well—she'd rather not think about the events that drove her to the airport and then to the other side of the country. The second she came face-to-face with the boy from her youth—the one who'd been a bit of a geek back in the day, but still managed to invade her private thoughts at night—she knew what this reunion was really all about.

Sex.

Honestly, what else could it be? She'd caught the hunger in his glance when she'd exited the plane, noticed the way his eyes darkened as they traveled the length of her body, gazing at her like she was a tall glass of water and he'd been in the prairie sun too long. She also noticed his sidekicks, Coop and Mac, who were standing on the tarmac waiting for Julia and Jess—girls she knew from years ago and who had received the same invitation as her—to disembark. What kind of guys tracked down women from their past to offer them a free vacation without wanting something in return? None. She was used to a world of tit for tat and could only assume Jag wanted the former.

She barely knew Curtis Jagger back in high school, and she was a little shocked to discover that he'd brought her here to live out some juvenile fantasy with her. In their teens, they'd traveled in different circles, and even though the president of the audiovisual club had grown into a gorgeous man with a banging body, it didn't mean she was going to hang around and become his plaything for the next week. She was so done with men, and rocking the headboard a time or two—or ten—with Jag was the last thing she needed right now. No matter how sexy he looked in that damn Stetson, or how long it had been since she'd been touched.

Don't even get me started on that.

What she needed to do was turn around, get on the next plane back home to Nova Scotia, and figure out what the hell she was going to do with her life.

Why would I want to do that? To run another political campaign for her fiancé? She snorted. What a way to put her hard-earned politics and international relations degree to use.

If only life came with a redo button. Even if it did, she doubted she could change hers, anyway. With a father who was mayor and a socialite mother who backed him unconditionally, she'd been groomed for the public life since the get-go.

Dammit, she was so tired of being a doormat, tired of doing what everyone else wanted her to do. She scuffed her Jimmy Choos on the barn floor as she paced. Maybe she should just say the hell with them all and stay here for a week and enjoy a few fantasies with the hot cowboy. What is that they say? An eye for an eye? Wouldn't that put her fiancé in his place?

Ex-fiancé.

With her back to Jag, she continued to pace, and a laugh caught in her throat, even though there was nothing funny about any of this.

"Hey," a deep, masculine voice said from behind. "You okay?"

Alix spun around, and when she found Jag watching her with rich, smoldering brown eyes, there was nothing she could do to stop her mind from traveling down an erotic path. One where limits were pushed, boundaries were crossed, and satisfaction was guaranteed. Her gaze traveled over his broad shoulders and wide chest, going lower to take in the jeans that hugged him to perfection. Her body stirred in a way it hadn't in so very long. Maybe having a wild week with him was exactly what she needed to do.

Except that is so not like me.

Or maybe it is, and I've just stifled that side of myself for far too long.

"Alix," Jag said again, taking a measured step toward her. "Relax. I promise you, everything is going to be okay."

With his hands shoved deep in his pockets, his grin was sexy and laid-back, but his easygoing nature did nothing to relax her. She sucked in a quick breath and ignored the need taking up residency between her legs as her voice lodged somewhere in her throat.

He slanted his head, his dark eyes full of heat and humor as they moved over her face. "You really don't remember me?"

"No," she lied, not wanting to admit to anything or let him think she was going to play into his fantasy. She cleared her throat and tried for normal. "Should I?"

He took another step forward, and apprehension surged inside her as the clean, spicy smell of his skin drowned out the aromas inside the barn. She filled her lungs with his scent. If he smelled this good, how would he taste? Her mind raced, envisioning her tongue on his hard body, licking, teasing, and savoring the saltiness of his skin. Oh God… Her sex clenched, and she shifted uncomfortably. In an attempt to take the edge off, she squeezed her thighs together, cursing her body for its unwanted reactions. When her attempts proved futile, she starched her spine and worked to purify her thoughts before she became completely unhinged.

What the hell is wrong with me?

"I used to sign the club's audiovisual equipment out to you back in high school," he explained. He watched her for a moment, like he was waiting for a lightbulb to go off inside her head. She folded her arms and stared at him, hoping to give him the impression that she had no idea what he was talking about. "That's okay," he said. "I'm not that guy anymore." He paused and pressed his thumb into a muscular chest that her traitorous fingers suddenly itched to touch. "I'd really like for you to get to know the guy I am today, anyway."

Too bad really, because the Jag from her youth was sweet and caring, always going out of his way to sign out expensive video club equipment to her when she needed it for one of her student council functions, or simply because she wanted to borrow it for her own personal use. But because he was from the wrong side of the tracks, and she had a reputation to uphold in society, her parents forbade her to associate with him, even though he was so much nicer than the privileged boys from her circle.

Tired of being yanked around by everyone in her life, she said, "No games, Jag. Tell me why you really invited me here." She held his gaze and smoothed down the bodice of her designer dress that belonged nowhere near a ranch, but she'd raced to the airport so fast she had no time to go shopping for something more appropriate.

"We were sort of friends once and I was thinking about you a few weeks ago." He gave a casual shrug. "I thought we could reconnect, get to know each other better." His lips twitched, but there was something very honest and open in his eyes as he looked at her.

"How will we do that?" she asked bluntly.

He waved his arm toward the towering Rocky Mountains with all their riding trails. "Ride the trails, go rock climbing, swimming. Whatever you want," he said.

She was no fool—or maybe she was. Either way this was about sex. And as tempting as his offer sounded, she couldn't do this. She had obligations and responsibilities. As the mayor's administrative assistant and daughter, she had duties to uphold at home and shouldn't have run off without letting anyone know. She shook her head. Dammit, she never should have tucked tail and gotten on that plane.

"I need to go home."

She stepped outside the barn and panned the huge estate. God, it really was beautiful, but she didn't belong here. No more than he belonged at one of her political functions.

As the midday heat engulfed her, she folded her arms to shade her pale, unprotected skin. *Wouldn't Mother have a fit if she knew I was standing in the sun unprotected?* She could almost hear the lecture now. *Appearances are everything, Alix.*

"When is the next plane?" she asked.

Instead of answering, Jag stepped up behind her, pulled

off his Stetson, and settled it on her head. Shaded by the wide brim, she lifted her head and looked into his eyes. She was about to thank him, but the second their gazes collided she caught the heat and hunger in his eyes. Every reason she had for leaving suddenly seemed so insignificant.

He squinted against the sun, all traces of humor gone from his face. "Why did you come?"

Angry tears pricked her eyes as she thought about the events that led up to this moment. She turned, offering Jag her back. She didn't want him to see her cry. Hell, the last thing she wanted to *do* was cry again. She pinched her eyes shut, but there was nothing she could do to expel the image of her fiancé kissing another woman.

There they were, arms around each other and lips locked in a way that left no mistake the two were lovers—or that she was pregnant. Yeah, she saw the bump, the way his hand rested on it in a protective manner. Tucked under a towering tree, in a secluded area of the park, they hadn't seen her taking pictures at first. Alix had been snapping photos of the sunset, enjoying nature at its best, until she spotted them. Her chest tightened, squeezing the air from her lungs. She'd never felt so betrayed, so used. If it weren't for her and her father's connections, Nelson wouldn't even be a member of the legislature.

Her hand went to her stomach. She'd been nothing but the dutiful fiancée and had given him everything she could. The one thing she couldn't provide, he went ahead and found with another woman. It was just last week they'd talked about the venue for their wedding. Did he really think he could have her and a mistress and child on the side? She wiped her face, swatting at the liquid on her cheek. The lying, cheating bastard didn't deserve her tears.

When his glance met hers, she should have confronted him. She should have smashed her camera over his head. But she ran home and swore off men as she threw her clothes in a suitcase. And now here she was, halfway across the country. Her life was a total freaking mess as she faced a man who'd always been so damn sweet to her—one who already had her reconsidering her vow to avoid the opposite sex. But wouldn't that just complicate her life more than it already was?

A strong palm landed gently on her shoulder and turned her around. "Why did you come?" he asked again, the tension between them palpable as he dipped his head to meet her gaze unflinchingly.

"I just…I was…" She exhaled slowly and looked at the ground. "Look, Jag, you asked the wrong girl for the wrong thing on the wrong day."

A rough, calloused hand cupped her chin and lifted it until she was looking directly at him. "I didn't ask you for anything."

She drew a shaky breath and eyed him suspiciously. "You just said you wanted us to get to know each other better, so I assume that this"—she stopped to wag her hand back and forth between them—"this setup is about sex. Some juvenile fantasy you must have been harboring about me." She shook her head, panning him from head to toe. "I mean, come on, look at you. Everything about you screams sex." As soon as the words left her mouth she gulped and tried to get them back. "Wait. I mean…" *Ugh.*

He grinned, but it wasn't conceited or egotistical. In fact, it was warm and tender, full of gentle understanding. She stared up at him. The Jag from her youth was no longer that awkward boy with a camera permanently strapped around his neck, nor did he wield his good looks and magnificent body like a weapon or think he was above reproach. He certainly wasn't a man from her world. Which made him that much more appealing.

Her purse began buzzing. She unzipped it and pulled

out her phone. Caller ID revealed it was her mother. She squeezed the phone until her knuckles turned white, and with eyes tired from all the tears she'd shed since catching Nelson, she stared at the screen.

"You don't have to answer it," Jag said quietly.

She grunted. If only he were right. But he just didn't understand how things were done in her world, especially with her mother. Dutiful daughter that she was, she slid her finger across the screen and tried not to sound as shaky as she felt. "Hi, Mom."

"Alixis, where are you?" she asked, her voice boarding on hysteria.

"I'm"—she paused and looked up to find Jag staring at her—"out of town. Visiting a friend."

"A friend? Who? Where are you?"

She pinched the bridge of her nose. She could only imagine what her mother would say if she knew she was here with Jag. Maybe she should tell her, and while she was at it, let her know she was thinking about having wild, crazy sex with him. Then again, she didn't want to send her into cardiac arrest.

"No one you know," she said.

"Nelson called and said you weren't home or answering his calls. He was very worried about you."

I just bet he's worried. About his career, her father's political pull—losing it all.

"I'm fine," she lied, pretty sure she'd never be fine again. A beat of silence reigned, then she asked, "Did he say anything else?"

"What else would he say?"

"Nothing," she said, feeling defeated. There was no point in saying anything. Her mother had stood in the shadows of her father's affairs, and likely expected Alix to do the same.

"Then get yourself home right now," she demanded,

her voice so loud she had to pull the phone away from her ear. "You know Nelson has that very important fund-raising dinner and speech tomorrow tonight. How would it look if you weren't by his side? And your father needs you in the office tomorrow. You have responsibilities. I don't know who you think you are, or what's gotten into you, but you can't just take off whenever you feel like it."

Her gut squeezed, the sense of duty that had been pounded into her since birth swimming to the surface. "I know. Okay—"

Jag moved closer, lightly cupped her elbow, and gave it a reassuring squeeze. "What do you want?" he asked.

Her words fell off as she took in the concern in his eyes. Oh God, he'd heard. Embarrassment clutched her, but as he continued to stare at her, he tightened his grip. Like a match to tinder, the strength of his touch, and the power behind it, sparked something inside her and set off a chain of events that filled her with rebellion.

What did she want?

How come no one had ever asked her that before? She rubbed one temple, feeling like she was carrying the weight of the world on her shoulders and that she could collapse at a moment's notice.

"Alix, I don't know what you're up to but it's your duty…"

There was that word again. "Duty." Except to her it wasn't just a word, it was the proverbial straw that broke the camel's back.

"I have to go," Alix said quietly, her calmness belying the storm going on inside her. Even though her mother was still lecturing, she powered down her phone. Much like an ostrich that shoves its head in the sand, she dropped her phone into her purse, zipped it shut, and ignored everyone and anything except this man staring at her. One who wanted to know what *she* wanted.

Jag rubbed her wrist with his thumb. "I want you to know, this week is about you. Anything you want, I can make happen. You're the one calling the shots."

She swallowed, hard. Her whole life she'd been a good girl, taught to behave in certain ways, inside the bedroom and out. But she was tired of that, goddammit, and maybe a week with the boy from the wrong side of the tracks was just what the good girl needed before facing her life back home. It wasn't like there could be more between them, or she'd fall for him in the end. They were different people from different worlds.

Am I really considering this?

She took a step back, from Jag and the whole situation closing in around her. "Well, you should probably know that I've sworn off men," she blurted out, still unsure about this whole setup. "In fact, I'm thinking about switching teams."

His grin widened, his dark eyes smoldering with passion and laughter as he raised his hands in surrender. "Okay. So you're playing for the other team now. That doesn't mean you can't hang out here and relax, does it?"

No, it didn't, and truthfully, she just couldn't face going home right now. She'd give herself this week, and then go back to her duties as a political daughter and administrator. Nelson, however, that was a different story. God, she'd been so stupid.

"I'll tell you what," he said, patience in his voice as his hands reached for hers. Every muscle in her body tightened. Would he be just as patient in the bedroom, taking his time to leisurely touch his woman's body, slowly building her climax, carefully, methodically bringing her higher and higher until she tumbled into a powerful orgasm? "Come tomorrow, if you want to leave, I'll make the arrangements." He dipped his head, a mischievous gleam in his eyes. "But if you change your mind and decide to stay, I promise to make it worth your while."

Even though she'd already made the snap decision to stay, she clamped her mouth shut, wanting to hear what Jag had planned for her. "Worth my while?" How intriguing.

"Maybe I can rustle up a few cow*girls* who can show you a good time."

With his mouth inches from hers, Alix swiped her tongue over her bottom lip and knew he could see right through her lie. From the way her body reacted to his closeness, everyone within a fifty-mile radius could tell how much she'd rather play with a sexy cow*boy*. He shifted closer, and when he aligned his body with hers, a warm shiver tingled all the way to her toes.

"In the meantime," he said, "why don't we take the horses out, and I can show you around." He gestured with a nod toward his camera case hanging on the hook inside the barn. "We can even take some pictures of the countryside, if you like." Heat moved into his eyes as they traced her face. "Or whatever else you'd like to take pictures of."

Alix's pulse leaped in her throat. But she quickly calmed herself, her heart settling back to a steady rhythm. No way could Jag know that she did contract work for a photography studio, one that on the surface looked like any other business, but under the radar offered sensual photography to selective clientele.

He arched a questioning brow. "You still enjoy photography, don't you?"

She bit back a moan and hoped like hell he couldn't see her body's reaction as she thought about the kind of photography she enjoyed. "Yes, but—"

"So what do you say then? Want to go for a ride with me?"

Ride? Need gathered in the pit of her stomach. What the heck was going on with her? She struggled to make sense of her reactions to him. How could she be thinking about sex with Jag after finding out her fiancé had cheated on her, and had a baby on the way?

Because you never loved him. Because you're tired of being an obedient daughter and fiancée. Tired of always doing what everyone else expects of you, never calling the shots yourself.

But wasn't this laid-back cowboy giving her the opportunity to do just that? If she did, would he judge her? Or would he push her and encourage her to be herself around him?

With the warm summer sun beating down on them, Jag looked over the beautiful but far too tense woman standing before him. Everything from the way the mayor's daughter dressed to her rigid body language told him so much about her. She was cultured and elegant, yes, but that put-together, outward appearance was merely a disguise, one that hid who she truly was.

Back in high school, he caught glimpses of the real Alix, a girl who was only allowed to associate with people from her parents' social circle. But now that he'd grown into a man with a successful career, he hoped she would look at him differently, give him a chance, and see that they might be good together.

At least I think we'd be good together.

A horse behind him whinnied, and he asked, "Have you ever ridden before?"

Her head jerked from side to side, his big hat swaying back and forth, making her look so adorable. "No. I always wanted to, but my mother thought horses were dirty creatures."

Jag looked at her clothes. With sleeves that reached past her elbows and a dress that dipped below her knees, she was hardly outfitted for cowboy country. "Did you bring anything suitable?"

She crinkled her nose and looked herself over. "What do you consider suitable?"

"Come on, I'll show you." He captured her hand in his, and she stiffened slightly. Was she having second thoughts? He hoped not, because she obviously needed this vacation. He'd heard both sides of the phone conversation, and seen how crushed she looked as her mother pushed her around like she was nothing more than a pawn in a game of chess, and it was all he could do not to punch something. She didn't deserve to be treated like that. Even if nothing more developed between them, he was glad he invited her, because she needed to let off some steam. Jag turned to her. "Alix," he whispered in a soft voice. "Nothing will happen here unless you want it to, and besides, you already told me you were playing for the other team. Let's just enjoy the day. And like I said, tomorrow if you want to leave, you can. Okay?"

"Okay," she said, and as she exhaled, he watched her visibly relax.

"Your luggage has been brought to your room. Let's go see if you have something you'll be comfortable riding in. If you don't, we can run into town and get you something."

She opened her mouth like she wanted to say something more and then shut it again. Instead of pressing, Jag led her into the lodge. A few minutes later, he stood near her door while she rooted through her suitcase. She pulled out a pair of knee-length shorts and a white, long-sleeved blouse, then disappeared into the bathroom. She came back a few minutes later and held her arms wide.

Her eyes were hopeful as she smiled up at him. "This should work."

Jag touched the sleeve on her blouse. Despite the air-conditioned room, her cheeks turned a pretty shade of pink.

His gaze panned her face, and he breathed in the sweet, clean smell of her skin before settling on her big blue eyes. He dipped his head and asked, "Do you love this shirt? Is it a favorite?"

She shook her head. "It's a shirt."

He gripped the sleeve, and with one quick tug, ripped it from the seam. A gasp sounded in Alix's throat as the fabric gave way, and her eyes widened.

"This will be much cooler," he explained.

She nodded, and after he ripped the other sleeve free, he stood back to admire the beautiful body she always went to great pains to cover.

He walked to the bed, grabbed his Stetson, and put it back on his head. "You'll need a hat."

"I have one." Excitement lit her face as she riffled through her suitcase and pulled out a wide-brimmed sun hat that could shade the entire ranch. "See!"

"Good." Jag bit back a grin as his gaze panned her pale skin. Did she ever go outdoors?

He took the hat from her and placed it on her head, but it caught on her ponytail. She reached around, and instead of releasing it and letting her curls fall down her back, she tightened it and stuck her hair under her hat. Too bad. He wanted to see it loose. Wanted her to relax.

As a private investigator, it was his job to understand people, and sweet Alix was desperate for freedom—from her family, her duties, and her conservative self. Her needs and sexuality bubbled beneath the surface. She was drowning in it, and if she didn't release it soon, let it break free, it would damn well suffocate her.

The lack of conviction in her voice when she insisted on returning home said she wanted to stay. The way she flushed when he moved close suggested he was part of the reason. She wanted to play, and he wanted to be her favorite toy. And those photos she took in the back room of the studio where she worked… Yeah, he knew all about her naughty hobby. All she needed was the right playground to help her open up to him, and he knew just the place.

He grabbed her hand, need propelling him into action. "Come on, let's go."

Thirty minutes later, after saddling a horse for Alix and giving her a quick lesson on riding, he hopped on his stallion and guided her toward the horse trails. He shot her a glance and could tell she was nervous but trying to hide it.

"You're a natural," he said in a bid to relax her.

"And you're a liar."

Jag laughed, and it brought a smile to her pretty face. "Come on." He snapped his reins and set his horse into a trot. He kept a careful eye on her as he led her along the river. The overgrown trees fringing the path provided an overhead canopy and offered them some much-needed shade. They entered a clearing, and Jag nodded to one of the ranch hands as a group of guests looking for a bona fide Old West experience pitched their tents and prepared for a night under the stars.

"Hey, Colt," Jag said, thinking about the time he'd helped his buddy out on one of his weekend excursions. Christ, that was a night to remember: too much drink, too many women, and a morning he could've done without. But Colt was a good guy who taught Jag a few things about being a cowboy and made sure the guests left satisfied, especially the female ones who were here for a real Western experience with an authentic cowboy.

While Jag enjoyed his bachelorhood, and the ladies, he was damn tired of waking up with a random girl in his bed. Casual sex had lost its appeal, and he wanted more, needed more, which was why he'd invited Alix here for the week. He might not come from her circle, but he'd always been attracted to her. Back in the day, they chatted when he was setting up the equipment for her meeting or taking it down. Things had always been so easy between them, and despite hanging out with a group of stuck-up girls who wouldn't dare give him the time of day, she'd always been kind to him, always so grateful when he helped her. Did they have a future together, or was he trying to rekindle something that existed only in his mind?

His glance roamed to her ring finger, taking in the circular indent. When he and his buddies, Coop and Mac, all co-owners of the ranch, had tasked his junior investigator with finding the three women from their past that they'd regretted letting go, the first report that came back said Alix was engaged. Jag had immediately pulled back. He'd be damned if he was going to home in on another man's woman, no matter how much he thought about her over the years.

But when his investigator went on to further report that her fiancé was cheating on her, it had changed the game plan, and he had gone ahead and sent the invitation.

Even though he hadn't known her as an adult, his protective instinct had kicked in. She didn't deserve that type of treatment. She was a kind, hardworking soul, always had been. The fact that she didn't wear her engagement ring and swore off men clued him in that she'd discovered the bastard was cheating.

He fisted his hands. While he'd like to beat the shit out of the guy for hurting her, he was glad she'd found out who he really was before going through with the wedding. And it gave Jag the opportunity to show her how a woman should really be treated, inside the bedroom and out. Where things went from there, time would only tell.

"Jag," Colt greeted in return before sticking a blade of grass between his teeth.

Alix slowed her mare beside him, and Colt arched a curious brow, intrigue brewing in his eyes as he turned his attention to her.

"Is your little lady here looking for an *authentic* Old West experience?" He gave Jag a wink, no doubt thinking back to the women the two had shared on that wild weekend. "'Cause you know, I'm just the guy who can give it to her."

Alix's eyes widened, her glance going back and forth between Colt and Jag. She was a smart girl. No doubt she caught Colt's sexual innuendos. "I—uh—no—"

"Alix, this is Colt. Stay away from him. He's trouble," he teased as he met Colt's glance. "And for the record, any experience she wants, I can give to her."

Colt laughed. "Well, you can't blame a guy for trying now, can you?" Colt tipped his Stetson and winked at Alix, his voice full of humor and heat. "Nice meeting you, ma'am. And remember, if you want to learn the ropes from a *real* cowboy, you know where to find me."

Grinning, Colt walked away. Jag gave a slow shake of his head and turned to Alix, who was watching the guests pitch their tents. He studied her for a moment, took in the childlike bewilderment in her eyes. Holy shit. "You've never been camping before, have you?"

She crinkled her nose. "That obvious?"

He nodded and tugged on the reins to get closer to her. "Seems like there are a lot of things you haven't done."

She shrugged one shoulder. "Been busy."

He made a clucking sound with his tongue. "You know what they say about all work and no play."

She looked down, a deep sadness on her face. "That's me, dull."

His heart squeezed. Shit, he hadn't meant to make her feel unhappy. "Hey, you're far from dull, Alix," he said softly. She blinked up at him. "You just forgot how to have fun." She swallowed, and as her eyes flitted over him with something that looked like want, he grabbed his canteen. "If you want, I can help you with that."

"What are you suggesting?" she asked, and he smiled. He loved her direct questions.

He unscrewed the cap and handed it to her. She opened her mouth to swallow, and his pants grew tight as he visualized those plump lips on his body.

"Well, you did mention you were playing for the other side, right?"

"Yes," she said, still sticking to that story.

He rested his hands on his saddle horn and looked into the distance. "Well, if you're open to exploring something a little different, I know a place."

She handed the canteen back to him, and he took a long pull.

Her face tightened warily, and she went quiet for a moment before saying, "I'm not sure."

As her good girl warred with her need to let go, he held his hands up. "Hey, no pressure. It's my job to make sure the guests have a good time and I just thought if you were curious…"

She angled her head, intrigue dancing in her eyes. "This place you're talking about—"

"It's a private ranch where cow*girls* go to play," he said.

The pulse at the base of her neck jumped and her breath came quick. "Oh."

"I just thought—"

Her chin tipped, a spark in her eyes he'd never seen before. "You thought right."

His head came back with a start and his cock thickened at the visual. Holy shit. Was she serious? He might want her in his bed, but if she wanted to experiment with the other team it would be wrong of him to stop her, right? His dude ranch catered to its guests' needs and really, it was the honorable thing to do, and had nothing to do with him wanting to watch or anything.

Yeah, sure.

He coughed to hide his arousal. "Then let's go."

They rode for another hour, stopping to take in the scenery and snap a few pictures on the way to his destination.

As he approached the nearby property, the neighboring lodge coming into view, he slowed his horse. Alix came up beside him and gazed at the ranch overlooking the river.

Equal amounts of curiosity and fascination flashed in the depths of her eyes. "Where are we?"

Before Jag could answer, the front door to the lodge swung open and sweet Katy O'Grady stormed onto her porch, shotgun aimed.

Alix tightened, but Jag grinned and held his hands up in surrender. "Put down the gun, Katy. It's just me."

With the sun in her eyes, Katy kept the gun aimed his way. "Jag, is that you?"

He trotted closer so she could get a better look at her two trespassers. "Yeah, it's me."

Katy dropped the weapon to her side. "You know better than to sneak up on me like that. I damn near shot you." She shook her head in amusement and added, "Get on in out of the heat, you two, and join me on the back deck for a glass of lemonade."

"What's going on?" Alix asked, nervousness lacing her voice.

"She gets a lot of intruders. A lot of the local teenage boys try to sneak on her land for a peek."

"A peek?" She frowned and looked around at the corrals and mountains, confused. "What exactly are they peeking at?"

He tossed her a grin and said, "Come on, I'll show you."

Chapter Two

They settled the horses, and Katy led them to the back deck. Alix sat next to Jag at a large round table overlooking the river. She shifted her chair to keep out of the sun as she glanced around, but then her gaze stopped abruptly. What the hell? She gulped air. When Jag said this was a place where cow*girls* went to play, he wasn't kidding. Even though he'd prepared her, nothing could have readied her to see two girls kissing in the river below. Sure, she photographed passionate couples in the private room of the studio, but this, well, this was unlike anything she'd seen through the lens of her camera.

A warm summer breeze filled with the scent of flowers washed over her but did little to cool down her overheated body. Of course, she wasn't serious when she told Jag she was switching teams, but damned if he wasn't playing a game with her…testing her by bringing her here.

She shot a glance Jag's way. She expected to see him watching the girls, but instead found his gaze riveted on her. The pulse at the base of her neck fluttered. With his long legs spread out before him, he sipped his lemonade and continued to stare at her. He was waiting for her reaction, waiting for her to do, say something. It made her want to shock him—tease and torture him sexually.

Good God, what has gotten into me?

As Katy stepped into the lodge, Alix shifted closer to Jag. "I've never been to a place like this before."

He leaned toward her, his glance moving over her face, everything in his closeness telling her he felt her apprehension. "If you don't like it here, we can leave. You're calling the shots."

A little astonished and maybe even a little thrilled at how in tune he was with her feelings, she took another glance around, and could almost hear her mother's voice in her head warning her to flee. She mentally put her fingers in her ears and hummed *lalalalala.*

She arched a brow and countered boldly, "I never said I didn't like it." Holy hell, whatever possessed her to say that? How, in the span of only a few short hours, was she able to turn her back on her strict upbringing and follow her own intuition? Perhaps it was because she was totally fed up with the facade, completely and utterly ready to break free and start pleasing herself instead of always pleasing others. Or perhaps it was because of Jag, his casual demeanor, and the way he could put her at ease with a simple word or glance. Either way, something inside her was beyond anxious to explore something new and see how the rest of this day, and week, all played out.

Jag grinned at her, and she relaxed a little. She grabbed her drink and used her finger to follow the drop of moisture dripping down the glass. He adjusted his pants, and she bit back a grin. Well, well, looks like two could play his game. She ran small circles around the bead, sinuously twirling her thumb closer and closer.

She watched Jag's Adam's apple bob as he swallowed.

"Why did you bring me here?" she asked, even though she knew he was pushing her to admit her needs—to herself.

His lopsided grin was slow, sexy, daring. "Like I said. You're a guest at my ranch, and because you're under my care, it's my job to understand all your needs and see to it that you leave satisfied."

She waved her hand toward the activities taking place in the water and then shot him a look. "And you think this satisfies my needs?"

Humor backlit his gorgeous eyes. "You were the one who told me you'd sworn off men and wanted to start playing for the other team. I'm here to make that happen." His tone was playful, yet challenging.

Her blood pulsed hot, and even though she didn't want to talk about her fiancé, something about Jag made her want to open up. "Do you want to know why I said that?"

He evaded her eyes and brushed his hand over the wooden rail. "If you want to tell me."

Alix opened her mouth, but then stopped. She eyed him. Oh my God, he knew! He already knew. She shook her head. "You already know, don't you?"

His nod was slow, his eyes somber when he said, "Yeah."

"How?"

"I'm a private investigator."

Understanding dawned in small increments. "So that's how you tracked down Julia, Jess, and me after all these years."

He scrubbed his chin. "That's right."

She narrowed her eyes, curious about him and his choice of careers. "What's your area of specialty?" Who knew the Jag from her youth would become a private investigator? She wrapped her brain around that and chalked it up to one more surprise to add to her eventful day.

"I catch cheaters," he answered, his tone a little too dark, a little too dangerous.

A flurry of emotions moved over his eyes, and a knot tightened her stomach. Had something from his past led him into that kind of work? "It must be hard…you know… confirming someone's suspicions."

He fisted his hands, his back stiffening. "Most already know, which is why they seek me out in the first place. But yeah, it's never easy."

A frown tugged at his mouth, and her heart pinched. How could she not like a guy who seemed to hate cheaters every bit as much as she did? She exhaled slowly and thought about Nelson. Anger churned in her gut. But deep inside, she knew catching him was a blessing. The discovery sent her straight into the arms of a man who seemed to care about what she wanted, and would, undoubtedly, go to great measures to give it to her.

Katy came back outside. Dressed in a long, loose dress, with her pretty blond hair tied back, she sat down next to them, her glance moving over Alix.

She zeroed in on the camera strung around Alix's neck. "We don't allow pictures, sweetheart. You can look all you like, and you can even play, but what happens here stays here."

"Oh, I wouldn't dream of it," Alix said, removing the camera. "I didn't even know about this place."

"Really?" Katy pursed her lips and went thoughtful for a moment. "Then why did Jag bring you here?" Green eyes studied Alix carefully and then slid to Jag.

"She's thinking about playing for the other team," he explained, his eyes never leaving Alix's as he tapped a finger on the wooden railing. "And I wanted to make sure she was properly cared for during tryouts." His gaze moved over her face before turning to Katy.

"I see," Katy said thoughtfully, looking back at Alix.

As if on cue, two girls came out from inside the lodge. Dressed in skimpy bikinis, they bounced across the deck, their eyes lighting on Jag.

"Hey, Jag," one of the girls said as she hopped on over to plunk herself down on his lap. She wiggled on his thighs, her breasts only inches from his mouth as the other girl came up to stand behind him. Alix shifted and smoothed her hand over her hat. Who were these women, and how did Jag know them so well? Had *he* played with them? An unexpected pang of jealousy hit out of left field. What the hell? Who Jag slept with was none of her business. He wasn't hers and she wasn't his and this week was about exploring fantasies and nothing else.

"Taylor," he greeted, and then looked over his shoulder. "Amanda." He smiled at the two, then asked, "What are you ladies up to today?"

"Just relaxing," Taylor answered. "We're heading to Wrangler's later tonight. Maybe we'll see you there."

"Probably not tonight." His grin came slow when he met Alix's glance. "I'll be meeting up with Colt and his crew to treat Alix to an *authentic* Old West adventure. "

What? Alix stared at Jag. He planned to treat her to an authentic adventure? Wait! What exactly did he mean by "authentic"? She wasn't sure, but given what he'd just introduced her to, who knew what was next. She was anxious to find out.

"So Jag, what brings you out here today?" Taylor asked as Amanda took a seat next to Alix.

While Jag explained the situation to Taylor, Alix smiled at Amanda, her body tense as she took in the other woman's near nakedness. Looking for a distraction, Alix reached for her lemonade, but with hands that were too shaky, she knocked the glass over.

Alix jumped from her chair as the cold drink spilled onto her lap. "Oh, damn. I'm so sorry." She grabbed a napkin and dabbed at the liquid, but it soaked through her shorts. She pressed it against her zipper. "I need to get cleaned up."

In the span of a second, Jag stood behind her, his mouth close to her ear. "I'll take you back."

"No need to rush away," Taylor said. "We can rinse your clothes here and I'm sure I have something that will fit you."

Alix spun to glance at Jag and noted the way his gaze had dropped to the hand rubbing her shorts. Typical male. Honest to God, if he didn't close his mouth he was going to swallow that fly buzzing around his head. She was about to decline their help and head back to her horse, but a wave of boldness swept through her when she caught the heat in Jag's eyes. Maybe she'd give him a run for his money as he pushed her to explore her needs.

And maybe this isn't all about him.

"Okay," she said. "If it's not a problem, maybe I should get out of these clothes."

Air rushed from Jag's lungs, a telltale sign that he was excited by the prospect. In a teasing manner, she wiggled out of her clothes, keeping on her bra and panties, which could easily pass for a bathing suit.

"Where can I rinse them?" she asked Katy.

"I'll take care of that for you."

Amanda captured her hand. "Why don't we jump in the water and get you rinsed off while Katy washes your clothes?"

Had Jag just groaned?

As she warred with the morals that had been pounded into her head since birth, her instinct was to run the other way, turn from the hedonistic acts, but she couldn't deny that this situation was exciting. And damned if she didn't want to challenge and tease Jag a little in return.

"Go on," Katy said. "I hate to see you ride all the way back in a sticky mess."

She removed her hat, and despite her mother's voice in the back of her head, warning her to keep out of the sun, she took a moment to enjoy the warm rays on her face.

Alix stole a quick look at Jag before leaving the deck. What was it about the heat in his eyes that turned her knees to pudding? A quick nod and then she turned her attention to the stairs to negotiate them carefully.

She watched Amanda, the taller cowgirl with the dark hair, bounce down the steps. They all reached the water and the two naked women swam to a nearby wharf. No wonder all the neighboring boys tried to sneak onto the land. Warmth gathered at her core and she adjusted her bikini panties over her groomed sex. *Groomed sex.* Hmph. What a waste of time that was. Her fiancé never liked to go down on her. Truthfully, sex with him had been fast, dull, and over before she ever reached climax. Sure, the doctor said her tipped uterus reduced her chances of getting pregnant significantly, but she was beginning to believe she couldn't have kids because Nelson rarely touched her. Abstinence is 100 percent effective in preventing pregnancy.

Probably didn't have the energy after—no. She wasn't going there. Not today. Today was about freedom.

Putting her ex out of her mind, she dipped her toes into the water to test it, unable to recall the last time she'd let her hair down and played. Taylor enthusiastically rushed past her, going thigh-deep as she splashed water in Alix's direction.

"Get out here, you two," Taylor said.

Finding the girl's energy contagious, Alix couldn't help but smile as she waded out, Amanda staying close beside her. When they reached Taylor, Amanda dipped low to soak her body, her long dark hair, now wet from the river, cascading down her back.

"It's so refreshing," Amanda said, her plump lips curling upward. Alix dipped lower, but when she felt cold water fall over her breasts, she yelped.

Taylor laughed and cupped her hands to pour the cool river water over Alix's body to rinse it. Amanda joined in, both girls splashing water over her and laughing as Jag watched from the deck. She touched herself, running her hands over her body, not really to rinse it, but because she liked the idea of him watching.

She stilled at that admission and looked up at Jag as he stood. The instant her eyes met his, heat moved through her.

Amanda nodded toward Jag. "Looks like your cowboy is waiting for you. You should head on up."

"Jag is a very patient man," Amanda added, her eyes twinkling. "But something tells me that when it comes to you, even a patient man has his limits." She turned from Alix and said, "Besides, Taylor and I are going to take a swim."

When the two women touched each other intimately, Alix nodded in understanding. Her weak legs carried her the few feet to the shoreline. At the top of the stairs, she found Jag waiting for her.

"Hey," he said, his voice deep and husky with desire.

"Hey," she returned breathlessly.

"So what do you think, Alix?" he asked, his voice rough with desire. "Have these cow*girls* given you what you needed to make the switch?"

She frowned, her gaze moving over his face before dipping lower to take in the hard ridge pressing against his pants. Her body came alive. Yeah, there was no way she could ever switch teams. Not when she craved the taste, texture, the hard length of a man inside her — the hard length of Jag inside her. And judging by that impressive bulge, he had a whole lot of length to give.

"It's tough to make that call," she said, her desire for him making her bold, urging her to try new things. With him.

He ran his thumb along her jawline, and she shuddered. Heat moved through her, the warmth of the sun nothing in comparison with the warmth of his touch. "Why is that?"

Feeling bolder than she ever had before, she lifted her

chin a little higher and said, "Because I've never been with a real cow*boy*, and I believe I should sample one before committing to one team, don't you?"

"Yeah, I do." He stepped close, his body crowding hers. "And I can help you out with that."

Heart beating wildly, she poked her finger into his chest and said, "That's what I was counting on, cowboy."

Chapter Three

Jag couldn't believe how fast Alix had loosened under his watchful eye. He didn't want to push too fast or too soon, but taking her to Katy's had been one hell of a good move. He'd watched as she touched herself in the water. At first, he thought she was doing it to tease him. But then their eyes met and he saw what was really going on. Sweet little Alix might like to watch others, but she also had exhibitionist tendencies. Damned if his day wasn't getting better and better.

After Katy's he'd taken her back to her room to get changed, and now here they stood, high on the mountaintop overlooking the ranch below, him tending to the horses and her trying to put a tent together as Colt took the others off on a hiking excursion.

"They didn't teach this in political science," she grumbled as she sorted through the poles.

He laughed as he finished with the horses. "Need some help?"

She bent to pick up the instructions, put her hand on her waist, and jutted one hip out as she read. He nearly swallowed his tongue. Jesus, she was sexy, and he wanted her in the worst way, but she'd been hurt and he needed to be careful. She thought this week was about sex, and while he wanted her underneath him—hell, he was a red-blooded male—he also wanted to build things slowly and see if there could be more between them.

But fuck, if she kept twisting and turning and bending over like that, he was going to lose his shit big-time.

She dropped the paper and grabbed the ropes, tangling herself in them. Instead of helping, he pulled his camera from his bag and snapped a picture of her. Her head jerked up.

"What are you doing?" she asked, blowing a loose strand of hair from her mouth.

He grinned and snapped another picture. "What does it look like?" he asked as her body stiffened.

"Don't take my picture," she said, her breathing changing slightly.

He bit back a wry grin, loving the fire in her eyes. "Why not?"

"I don't like it." Despite her protest, he took another one. "Jag, don't."

"What, you like to take sexy pictures of others, yet you don't like to be photographed yourself?" he asked, deciding to push her just a tiny little bit. A flush crawled up her face, and when she didn't answer he added, "If you ask me, I think you like to be watched as much as you like watching."

Her eyes widened as she stared at him, and the hunger inside him nearly consumed him as heat backlit her baby blues.

Snap.

"Jag—" she began, sounding even more breathless as she tried to untangle herself. "How did...how do...?"

Snap.

Her chest rose and fell erratically, the rope tightening on her breasts.

Snap.

"Tell me something."

"What?" she asked softly, like she could no longer fight the desire rising in her.

"When you touched yourself in the water today, did you like me watching? Is that something that turns you on, baby?" She hesitated and averted her eyes. "Do you trust me, Alix?"

Her gaze shot to his. "I…I do."

"Good. Then I want you to be honest with me, but more importantly I want you to be honest with yourself."

She darted a glance around the clearing and answered quietly with, "Yes."

Snap.

"If you liked it, we could do it again." He struggled to keep his voice level, keep a measure of calm when all he wanted to do was toss the camera and take her the way he wanted to.

It's too soon, dude.

Her throat worked as she swallowed, and she freed her hands, leaving her capable of fleeing and putting a stop to this game if she wanted to.

As fire raged between his legs, he pushed her even more. "If you want to touch yourself, I could watch."

Equal amounts of heat and nervousness stole over her face, and she stood there staring at him. Damned if she wasn't debating her next move. A branch cracked nearby and her eyes widened. She peered into the surrounding woods and went quiet, thoughtful, like she was waging some internal war.

"What if someone…"

Jag scanned the woods, but there was no one around. "If there is someone out there, maybe you'd like it if they watched, too."

A low, sexy moan caught in her throat. Christ, he couldn't wait to explore all her needs. "Jag."

Snap.

He took his sweet time to tease her, wanting to draw out this verbal foreplay, because well, it was fun, for both of them. "I'd really love to see how you touch yourself when you're alone. That is if you want me to."

She visually quivered.

Snap.

She stood still for a long moment, heat coloring her cheeks. "Touching myself in front of someone is…"

"Something that turns you on?" he asked, finishing her sentence.

"Yeah," she said, her voice a breathless whisper.

"If you're open to exploring, we can. Totally up to you. You're the one in charge here."

Her chest rose and fell. Was she considering it? Jesus, he sure as hell hoped so.

"What do you say, sweetheart, are you up to trying something new?"

They exchanged a long, heated glance, and then instead of answering, her hands went to her blouse. She toyed with the button.

Snap.

She wet her lips, and his cock jumped.

Snap.

Long fingers peeled open her blouse. Her lids drifted down as she lifted her breasts from the cups. She kneaded her tender flesh, soft moans escaping her throat.

"Open your eyes," he said.

Her lids fluttered back open, and his jaw clenched when she pinched her nipples, rolling those gorgeous, hard buds like they were starved for attention.

Snap.

He watched her play with herself as his cock pressed painfully against his jeans. He choked back a groan. "Is there anything else you'd like to show me?"

Her grin turned naughty as she slid her hands lower.

Snap.

She released the button on her shorts. He drew in a breath as he throbbed, calling on his patience.

With the forest hugging them, he stepped closer, and he could almost hear her purr as she shimmied out of her shorts. She peeled off her panties and stood before him in nothing but her open blouse, with her breasts spilling from her bra.

"You have a beautiful body, Alix. Why do you always keep it covered?"

"The mayor's daughter doesn't show any skin," she answered, her voice husky.

"I'd like to see your skin, every inch of it, actually." He took another step closer. Her eyes met his, and the desire reflecting there filled him with heat. He touched her chin, lightly brushing the rough pad over her silky cheek, and felt a tremble move through her. "Would you like to show me?"

Instead of answering, she slowly released the buttons on her blouse. With a little shrug it fell from her shoulders. A breeze rushed past and her nipples tightened behind her lace bra. She cupped her breasts and then fingered the strap, running her thumb up and down the silky length. A beat passed, a moment of hesitation. She glanced at him, her lashes blinking rapidly, her shyness warring with the need to pleasure herself.

"Beautiful," he murmured softly, being careful not to break the mood. "So incredibly sexy."

She sucked in a fluttered breath, his words turning her on and making her bolder. The rasp of her strap sliding down her arm reached his ears and thickened his cock, and when her hand went behind her to unhook her bra, exposing her beautiful breasts, he nearly bit off his tongue. Christ, she was so gorgeous, so exciting.

Lids languid with desire and mouth slack, she slid one hand down over the soft swell of her stomach. Wiggling her hips, she toyed with the band on her panties.

"Don't stop, sweetheart."

Air rushed from her lips as her hips stilled, her thumbs slipping under the thin lace. A quick tug and her panties were at her feet. She slowly lifted her legs to kick them away. Her hands crawled back up her thighs, lightly brushing her bare mound, a soft caress that brought color to her cheeks. He groaned, and her head fell back, a soft moan slipping out on a sigh of pleasure.

Fuck, he was so hard it hurt.

He pressed a button on his camera and propped it on his bag, keeping it focused on Alix. Then he came back to stand before her.

Jesus, he wanted her. "Tell me what you want."

He pushed his erection against her, to let her know how much he wanted her, and wanted this.

She lifted her chin, her eyes full of urgent need. "I want you to kiss me."

As her soft whisper curled around him, his muscles bunched, and his cock raged inside his pants. His mouth pressed hungrily to hers, taking full possession. The second he tasted her sweetness, a growl crawled out of his throat. The moan of pleasure seemed to do something to her, awaken something primal. She pressed against him, rubbing that hot, wet pussy of hers on his leg.

"I want you naked," she demanded. "I want to touch you."

Wanting—needing—that too, he stepped back and made short work of his clothes, leaving them in a pile in the grassy clearing. His erection jutted forward, and he wrapped his fingers around it to stroke himself.

Alix's eyes widened. Another first for her, he guessed. He stroked harder. "Oh God," she murmured under her breath.

Entranced by what she was doing and forgetting they were in a clearing, he shot a quick glance over his shoulder to ensure they were alone, then stepped beside her, touching her shoulder lightly to reposition her.

"Alix," he said softly. She lifted her eyes to his. He smiled and asked, "What do you want now?"

She reached out and placed her hand on his stomach, running it over his muscles, going lower and lower to the base of his cock. Her fingers closed around him, dragged up the length, then over his crown.

Fuck yes.

"This." She squeezed. "All of it. Inside me. Now."

He swallowed, and racked his brain to catch up as she stroked him.

She blinked up at him, desire swimming in her eyes. "And I want it hard."

Jesus.

His cock grew another inch. "Right here, where anyone can see?" he asked, teasing her fetishes.

"Yes," she answered and gestured toward the ground, her body trembling with need. "Right here, right now," she said, her words rushed, a new sense of urgency about her.

Needing to slow her down so he could make it good for her, he said, "Easy, baby."

"Please, Jag. It's been so long…"

What the hell? Christ, up until yesterday she'd been engaged. What kind of a man—lover—was he? But when she pushed against him, and he felt her wetness on his thighs, he couldn't think about that any longer.

He gripped her ponytail and gave it a tug, forcing her face up. His lips found hers again, and he took his time, tasting her sweetness before moving to the hollow of her throat. She quivered beneath his lips as his hands roamed her body, exploring and getting to know her every curve, her every lush contour, while he helped free her and show her that a sensual woman like her should never be subdued.

He cupped her breasts, and her head rolled back.

Desperate to taste her, he bent forward to wrap his mouth around one of her hard buds. "Jesus," he murmured as her pebbled nipple swelled inside his mouth. She writhed, and he struggled to take it slow.

"Jag, please…"

She was so fucking aroused it damn near killed him. He dropped to his knees, kissing the flat of her stomach as he slipped a hand between her legs, urging them apart. When she widened, he slid his fingers over the inside of her silky thigh, climbing higher and higher but never touching the spot that looked so swollen and achy for him. He loved how much she wanted it—wanted him.

"I need to get you ready, baby."

She rocked her hips, grabbed two fistfuls of his hair, and said, "I am ready."

He grinned up at her, noting the eagerness on her face, but there were so many things he wanted to do before he took her. "Poor baby, so needy. But don't worry. I'm going to make you feel all better."

A cry caught in her throat, and her hands went to her breasts as he widened her sex to find her wet. He lightly brushed her clit, and her hips jerked. Christ, she was so sensitive, so close to climaxing just from their camera foreplay.

He ran his hands over her flesh, taking his time to caress every inch of her as he savored her satiny warmth, taking her closer and closer to the precipice but never allowing her to tumble over.

"So good," she murmured. "Never been so good."

His heart hammered. Christ, he liked hearing that. Wanting to take the edge off before he drove into her, he sank his mouth into her warm, wet heat to give her a sample of the pleasure to come.

Her hands fisted his hair, and her body shuddered as he circled her with his tongue. Fuck, she tasted like sugar, cotton candy, and everything sweet. Everything about her syrupy nectar tested his restraint, and it took every ounce of control he had to fight the powerful urge to pull her onto his hips and fuck her hard.

He drew a ragged breath, and she moved, pressing against him, showing no qualms about what she wanted. "More," she cried out. "Hard, faster."

He pushed a finger inside her and found her so wet and tight. Jesus, he had no idea how much longer he could hang on.

She pushed against him, the look on her face almost frantic as she chased an orgasm, her body stiffer than it should be. He pumped in and out of her, wanting nothing more than to relax her, to help her loosen the reins and forget about everything except letting go—with him.

"That's it, baby. Take what you need."

The second the words left his mouth, he felt her muscles clench. A sexy bedroom noise crawled out of her throat as she clawed at his shoulders. He skimmed his lips over her stomach and held her to him as he stroked her clit harder, applying a touch more pressure to help end the sweet torment.

Her body shuddered. "That's my girl," he whispered as she cried out his name, loud enough that anyone in the vicinity could hear it. When her muscles clenched around him, his chest swelled, and he couldn't even put into words how fucking crazy it made him to see her like this.

No longer able to fight it anymore, and desperate to be inside her, he climbed to his feet, grabbed her by the waist, and lifted her onto his hips.

Her breasts crushed against his chest, moisture sealing their bodies as her lips found his. She kissed him passionately, deeply, her tongue slipping inside to play with his as he walked them backward toward the nearest tree.

Breathless, frantic to get inside her, Jag searched the ground for his jeans. He found them and rooted in the pocket for protection. "Shit, I can't find a condom." He scanned the ground. Had it fallen out?

A soft palm touched his face, and behind the fire in her eyes, he caught a hint of sadness. He stilled, his lust-rattled brain trying to sort out what was going on when she said, "It's okay, I'm clean."

"I'm clean, too."

"Then please, Jag. Just fuck me."

"You sure?"

"Positive."

"Good, because I don't want anything between my cock and you."

"Me neither." The heat behind those words nearly brought on his orgasm. He groaned loudly, scooped his shirt from the ground, and draped it over her shoulders before he pressed her back into the bark. Her chest rose, and her eyes filled with excitement as he secured her against the tree and kneaded her butt.

Her legs wrapped tighter around him. "I've never been fucked like this before," she said.

"I'm going to take you so many ways this week, you won't know up from down."

Her laugh was edgy, and she squirmed and said, "I'm looking forward to that."

So was he.

He pressed his mouth to hers and softly licked her lips as he drew her down lower on his hips, until his crown breached her tight opening. "You're so fucking hot."

She opened her mouth to say something, but her words were lost on a moan when he pulled her down harder, ramming his cock as deep as it would go.

"Oh my, yes," she cried out, her nails scratching at his back as he drove her against the tree, angling his body for better leverage.

Her body shuddered around his dick, forcing him to close his eyes in distress and get his shit together before he lost it. She bucked against him, demanding more. He pushed hard, faster, impossibly deeper.

"Yes, just like that."

As they came together as one, heat exploded inside him. He'd never felt anything so goddamn amazing. Her slick heat coated the length of him, the frictionless barrier driving him to the brink in record time. But it was too soon…too soon to lose control.

He tried to slow down, he really did, but patience was no longer an option, not when she was so hot, so wet for him, and begging him to fuck her. He pumped hard, ravishing her sweet pussy as he ground his pelvis against her clit. She moved restlessly, and he could feel her muscles tightening, squeezing the length of him in the most mind-fucking ways.

"I'm…I'm…" she cried out, and a second later, as she clenched around him, it pushed him to the point of no return.

Air rushed from his lungs, and his body stiffened. "Fuck," he cried out, struggling to hang on until she rode out the waves of ecstasy.

"Feels so good," she murmured.

"Alix," he mumbled, as a soft gasp broke from her lips and pushed him over the edge, and he pumped deeper, then stilled inside her. He held her tight, burying his face in her neck as he shuddered in surrender, depleting himself high inside her. His ragged moan echoed in the vast clearing, and somewhere overhead, birds took flight.

Sweat coated his body, his breathing labored as he remained inside her.

"That was good. No wonder women have cowboy fantasies," she murmured into his hair.

Jag inched back, smiling at the contentment in her eyes.

"That's it?" he teased, completely blown away by the sex.

"Just good?"

Her legs slid to the ground, and she returned his smile and teased, "Well, it's not like you're an *authentic* cowboy."

He laughed hard and said, "Tough audience."

As they stood there, streaks of pink and purple bruising the skyline, they basked in the glow of orgasm. Jag smoothed back the few loose strands of hair that had escaped her ponytail and met her glance.

There was a new seriousness in her eyes. "Actually, I didn't know it could ever be that good."

Neither did he.

Of course he knew it would be good with her, but he had no idea it could be *that* good. Christ, he'd never lost it so fast before, but watching her come undone for him pressed buttons he didn't even know he had. He sucked in air, but couldn't seem to refill his lungs. Even though he wanted to see if there could be more between them, what he was feeling right now was foreign, a little more than overwhelming. Jesus, he could barely think, let alone breathe. Her hand went to his face, her touch going right through him and scaring him a bit.

He struggled to pull himself together and asked, "So tell me, does this mean you've decided not to switch sides?"

"Actually, I'm still not sure." She crinkled her nose playfully, and he relaxed a little.

"No?"

"No," she answered, marching her fingers over his chest. "I'm still on the fence. God only knows what it will take to figure it out."

Grinning, Jag carried her to the sleeping bag and lowered her. He climbed on top, and as he pinned her beneath him, she gave an excited gasp.

He pressed his lips hard to hers, taking full possession of her body as he said, "God isn't the only one who knows what it'll take, baby."

Chapter Four

Alix took in the sleeping man beside her. There was so much more to the private investigator who liked to play cowboy on the weekends. Jag was an amazing man, but she wasn't going to fall for him. This week was just about fulfilling fantasies, and her body was all she could offer.

But still, she couldn't deny that last night he'd taken her beyond her wildest imagination and taught her so much about herself, so much about her ex and how little he cared about what she wanted. As long as she played the dutiful daughter and fiancée, everyone was happy. Well, everyone but her.

She touched Jag's face, lightly running her hand over the sexy stubble on his chin. Why had she ever stayed with a man who cared so little about her needs?

Because he was handpicked by your mother.

Jag stirred, and something warm flooded her veins. Even if she did want more from him, and she wasn't saying she did, they both lived very different lives. And sure, he was coaxing her to let go, but that didn't mean he wanted a future with her, right?

With dawn approaching, she climbed out of the sleeping bag, quietly unzipped the tent, slipped into her shoes, and stepped outside. Not wanting to wake the guests while they slept, she tiptoed to the edge of the clearing to look out at the ranch nestled in the valley far below. Fresh morning smells of grass and hay wafted before her nose, and the sounds of the wildlife stirring around her gave her a sense of peace. Even though she was alone, she didn't feel lonely. She was experiencing so many firsts here on the ranch with Jag.

The early morning sun climbed over the mountain, and as the warm rays of light touched her flesh, she fanned her hair out and exhaled slowly.

"Hey," a soft voice said from behind, jolting her out of her thoughts.

Jag.

Instead of turning, she stood there. The ground crunched beneath his feet as he came up behind her. Warm hands circled her body, and she exhaled slowly as he pulled her against his chest. She melted into him and scanned the gorgeous, sprawling expanse of countryside. As she basked in the quiet and harmony, the closeness she felt with Jag, she whispered, "I love it here." She felt Jag's heart beat against her back and reveled in the easy intimacy between them as he stroked her arms.

"So you'll stay for the week?" he asked.

She leaned into him. "Yes," she answered quietly, without hesitation. "There's nowhere else I'd rather be." It was true. She wasn't just staying because she had no idea where to turn. She liked being here, with Jag.

He spun her around, his dark eyes looking over her face. Worry pulled his brow into a vee. "Is everything okay?"

Her glance fell to his bare chest, noting the way his jeans hung low on his hips. "I'm just—I'm not sure I ever want to go back."

"Not ready to face what waits for you?"

"I know I'll have to eventually."

Jag gave a hard shake of his head. "Your ex is an asshole and a damn fool to cheat on a woman like you. Just so you know, I never would have sent you that invitation had I thought you two were happy and in love."

She looked down, her body stiffening as she considered the wasted years she spent helping Nelson build his political career when he clearly wanted her only for her connections and because she was loyal and dutiful.

When she went quiet, he tipped her chin, his eyes moving over her face. "Alix, do you still love him?"

"If I loved him, I wouldn't have done…" She paused and waved her hand toward the tent and said, "All the things we did."

His face relaxed. "Did you ever love him?"

"No, I don't think I did."

"Then why were you with him?"

"Because he fit my mother's criteria for a husband. Right family, right side of the tracks, right political career. No one outside her social circle was good enough for her only daughter."

She felt Jag stiffen beside her and suspected her words hit like a sucker punch. "I'm sorry. I didn't mean to suggest you weren't good enough."

"But wasn't that why you had nothing to do with me in high school?" he asked, calling her out.

"Yes." She placed her hands on his chest, emotions rising in her. "I guess what I'm trying to say is, her approval was always very important to me, but I don't like myself, Jag. I don't like the doormat I've become because of it."

"It's okay, I know deep inside you're not a product of your mother any more than I'm a product of my father." He raked his hands through his hair, and his voice dropped an octave. "To be honest, I'm kind of glad you avoided me in high school. I wouldn't have wanted to bring you around my place anyway. My father was a drunken, cheating bastard, who hurt my mother more times than I can remember. She didn't deserve that from him. She was the sweetest person. She was so good to me, Alix." His voice hitched when he said, "Even when she was hurting, she tried to hide it, and shelter me."

Her heart squeezed at the pain she heard in his voice. "I'm sorry."

"He resented her," he continued. "Resented having to stay because she got pregnant right out of high school. He forfeited a scholarship that was his ticket to a better life. He stayed behind and did what was supposed to be the right thing, but he grew to hate his life. He buried his sorrows in a bottle and in the beds of other women."

"Why did your mother stay?" she asked quietly, her heart tightening from the fact that he would share something so personal, so painful with her.

"She stayed because by the time she found out, she felt it was too late to get out or start over again, especially with a kid in tow. She turned a blind eye, even though it slayed her. I hate what he did to her."

"And to you."

He shrugged, but she knew his pain ran deep. "And that's why you became a private investigator specializing in infidelities."

"Yeah, I guess. I figure if I catch these guys early enough, I can prevent what happened to my mother. "

"Jag," she began. "You know, you're as sweet, kind, and caring today as you were all those years ago."

"Shhh," he whispered, his eyes glinting. "I have a reputation to uphold around here." When she chuckled, he squared his shoulders and shot her an accusing glare. "Hey, wait, I thought you said you didn't remember me."

She shifted from foot to foot and gave him a coy look. "Yeah, well, maybe I remember more than I admitted."

His mouth turned up at the corner, making him look boyish and adorable. "And maybe I know more than I admitted, too."

She caught a mischievous twinkle in his eyes and asked, "Oh, yeah? Such as?"

He tapped her nose. "Well, I remember the straitlaced, straight A, popular girl who was perfect by anyone's standards. But I knew her secret, something she kept from the entire world."

She bit down on her lip. He knew about her fetishes, but how? "How did you know?"

"Do you remember that day I came by your place to collect the camera you borrowed?"

Alix's mind raced back in time, remembering the day he'd shown up on her doorstep. "Yes," she answered.

His hands spanned her waist, and she never felt such an easy intimacy with anyone. "You answered the door in a short pink robe."

Her stomach quivered. Just before he'd arrived that day she'd been… "You…you knew what I was doing. How?"

"I saw you, baby. I heard strange noises as I cut through your backyard, and when I peeked through the fence and found you lounging by the pool, touching yourself as you flipped through pictures on your camera, I knew there was another side of you."

Her eyes widened in surprise. "You never said anything."

"I didn't want to embarrass you."

"Thank you," she whispered quietly. God, she would have been so mortified if he'd mentioned it to her back then.

She drew a breath, thinking about the sexy boudoir pictures she took at the studio. Heat moved into her cheeks.

Jag must have misread her reactions. He brushed his

thumb over her lip and said, "Hey, don't be embarrassed now."

"Actually, I'm not," she said, completely comfortable with Jag and becoming much more comfortable letting the other side of herself shine through. "But I'm wondering why you're telling me now."

"Because I want you to know you can be yourself around me, and I like that sexy side of you."

He gave her a warm smile that robbed her of her next breath and then looked past her shoulders. Heart fluttering, she turned to follow his gaze. In the valley below, she spotted Coop coming from the small cottage at the back of the lodge.

"Does Coop live in the cottage?"

"No."

She heard sadness in his voice and spun back to him. "What?"

He rubbed the stubble on his chin and said, "He doesn't like to talk about it, so this is between us, okay?" She nodded, and he continued. "He bought this ranch for his mother. She's the one who lives out back."

"Oh, wow, I had no idea. Wait, didn't you say you all owned it?"

"We do. His mother suffers from Alzheimer's, and he bought this ranch because she grew up on one, and it helps her feel more content. Coop couldn't afford it alone, so Mac and I went in on it with him."

A bone-deep warmth flowed through her. Honest to God, he was the sweetest guy she knew, and how she thought she could have sex with him without feeling something more was beyond her. She briefly pinched her eyes shut and pressed her fingers to her temples. Emotions were not a part of this fantasy.

Her throat tightened, and she struggled to speak. "Does Coop live here full-time?"

"No, he has a caretaker for his mother, but we fly out

whenever we can."

She exhaled slowly. "If I owned this place, I'd live here full-time."

"Really, you'd give up the rat race and move here?"

"Yeah, I would. I never wanted to be in politics, Jag."

He touched a strand of her hair, running it through his fingers. She shivered again, remembering the way he touched her body with those rugged hands of his. "What is it you wanted to do?"

"I wanted to be a teacher."

"What did you want to teach?"

"It didn't really even matter." Sadness moved through her. "I just love kids and love being around them."

"And now?"

She gave him a playful wink, not wanting to think about a life without her own kids. "Now, I think I'd like to be a cowgirl."

Jag laughed. "Well, you came to the right place for that. And wouldn't you just know it? We have children's camps here at the end of the summer. Cowgirl instructors are always needed. That would certainly kill two birds with one stone."

"What about you?"

"What about me?"

"Did you ever think about living here full-time?"

He shrugged easily. "Sure, I can work anywhere. I can hunt down cheaters in any city."

"Then why don't you?"

He pointed to the large homestead by the lodge. "Because that's a big old lonely house to be in by yourself. It needs kids, don't you think?"

"Yeah, I do."

She looked at the house and pictured herself living in it. She'd have to freshen up that paint, of course, and it really did need a little garden out back, and that rail, well, every child needed a rail to slide down and that one wasn't safe at all. She closed her hand over her stomach and felt a maternal pull. She quickly stopped herself from fantasizing. She couldn't have kids, and in less than a week she'd be leaving here, heading back home to pick up the pieces of her life and figure out what was next. Jag didn't exist in that reality, and she'd be wise to remember that.

"Hey, are you okay?" he asked, turning her to face him.

Concern danced in his eyes as they moved over her face. "Nelson wanted kids," she said, baring her soul. "I couldn't give them to him."

He feathered his thumb over her cheek, brushing away a tear. "Alix? What's wrong?"

"Last year the doctor said my chances of conceiving were slim."

"There are other ways to have children."

She snorted. "Yeah, like having sex with someone else?"

He frowned. "What?"

"Nelson wasn't just cheating, Jag. He had a baby on the way."

His eyes turned a darker shade of brown as he shook his head. "Nelson's an asshole. You do realize that, don't you?"

She nodded. "I don't know why I just told you that."

"Because he hurt you."

"Maybe," she said. "Or maybe because you're easy to talk to, easy to be with…easy to trust."

Her words seemed to trigger a reaction in him. He pulled her closer, and the tenderness that moved over his face did the strangest things to her insides. "He's never going to hurt you again, Alix. Not if I have anything to do with it."

She shook her head; the warmth and comfort he offered were like a healing balm to her soul. She snuggled into him. "It's strange, really. I'm more angry than hurt. Angry that I've wasted so many years on him, all because I needed to play the role my mother assigned to me."

He captured her hand. "Don't waste any more time thinking about him, not when there are so many other important things to think about."

"Yeah, like what?" She smiled up at him and felt a connection that went beyond their agreement of a weeklong affair. She'd crossed an imaginary line in the sand with him, and was treading on dangerous territory, one that could end in more tears.

This is so not good. So not good at all.

"Like me." He gave her a boyish, lopsided grin. "And all the things you want to do today."

"Okay."

A noise sounded, and they both turned to see Colt climb out of his tent. Looking rugged, sexy, and sleepy, he stretched out his arms, tossed a blade of grass into his mouth, and said, "Mornin'."

"Morning," she and Jag greeted in return. A second later, two Barbie-doll blond women dressed in sexy short shorts and bikini tops came crawling out behind him. With sun-kissed skin, collagen-pumped lips, and manicured nails that belonged nowhere near a ranch, they gave Jag a once-over.

Feeling a sting of jealousy, Alix said, "I think I need to go back to the lodge for a shower."

"That's what the river is for," Colt said.

"I think I've roughed it enough for one day," she responded as Jag pulled her tight against him, draping a possessive arm around her that made her feel cherished, special—something she'd never felt before. "I need a real shower."

"That's no way to get an *authentic* Old West experience. Isn't that right, girls?" Colt asked, grinning as the two women flanked him, touching his body intimately.

"No way at all," one of them cooed.

"Don't worry." Alix looked at Jag and exchanged a hot,

knowing look. "I'm getting all the cowboy experience a girl could ask for."

S ince this was a working dude ranch, Jag's chore for the day included leading a group of guests on a horseback-riding adventure. He'd cleaned himself up and grabbed a bite to eat, then met a ranch hand, Blake Callahan, inside one of the many barns. A half hour earlier, he'd left Alix in her room, giving her some time to herself, not only because she needed it, but because he needed it, too.

In the few short days she'd been here, she'd totally rocked his world. He had a feeling they'd be good together, but he was falling harder than he ever thought he could. Christ, if she left here without so much as looking back, it would kill him as quick as Katy's weapon.

"Hey," Blake greeted with a tip of his Stetson. "Thought we'd catch up with you at Wrangler's last night, but I ran into Taylor and Amanda, and they said you had your hands full."

Jag grinned. "You could put it that way."

Blake lifted a curious brow. "Oh yeah, who is she?"

Jag tossed his saddle onto his stallion and casually rolled one shoulder. "You wouldn't know her."

Blake shook his head. "Damn, there must be something in the water." He shook his canteen, then set it aside. "I think I'd better find something else to drink. Otherwise, I might end up whipped like you, Coop, and Mac."

Jag laughed. "There are worse things than being whipped."

"Well now, that depends on what kind of whipping you're referring to," he said in a lazy drawl. "The kind I'm referring to has a ball and chain attached."

"One of these days, Blake," Jag began as he finished saddling the stallion, "you'll find the right girl, and you'll know what it's all about."

"Well, until then, I think I'm just going to have me some fun." He gestured with a nod over Jag's shoulder. "Now there's a little filly who looks like she's ready for a good time."

Jag angled his head to see Alix. "She is, but not with you." He jabbed his thumb into his chest. "That filly is mine, and I'm not into sharing. Not anymore."

Turning from Blake, Jag walked to the doorway, wrapped one arm around Alix's waist, and dragged her close. Her body melted against his, and he planted a hard kiss on her mouth, letting Blake know in no uncertain terms that this one was a keeper, and his days of playing were over.

A catcall whistle came from Blake, and Alix pulled back. Confusion moved over her face. "What was that?"

"That, cowgirl," he said slowly, "was just the beginning."

"The beginning?"

"Yeah, once I'm done with my chores, I have a surprise for you."

"Oh, really?" Heat moved over her face, and he inched back when all the guests started filing into the barn for their afternoon ride. Then she crinkled her nose, like she just remembered something distasteful. "I don't like surprises anymore."

"Don't worry. You'll like mine."

He captured her hand and led her to the group gathering around the horses. After introducing himself and pairing everyone with their horses, Jag led them outdoors and nodded to Mac, who was in the corral teaching rope-tying skills. He slowed to let Alix catch up to him, and when he cast her a glance, his heart missed a beat. Her cheeks were flushed from the sun, her long hair flying haphazardly behind her. He noticed she wore a different pair of shorts and a new shirt, minus the sleeves.

She looked happy and content, her shoulders no longer

hugging her ears as she smiled at him. Cowboy country was good for her. It was for him, too. Which was why he wanted to live here permanently—with a big family. He rubbed the stubble on his face. Yeah, he had no trouble packing up and moving here full time. He had no folks or family back home waiting. Truthfully, the only things he had back in Nova Scotia were his pals, Mac and Coop, and they were here on the ranch nearly every weekend anyway.

The more he thought about it, the more the idea of living here full-time appealed to him. He already knew that distancing herself from those who tried to run her life, and finding her own path, was good for Alix, too.

But what did she want?

They spent the afternoon riding trails, stopping to refresh their horses and drink from their canteens at the river. Alix snapped pictures along the way, capturing couples stealing kisses during their adventure. A long while later, on their return home, he noticed she seemed a bit uncomfortable. He slowed his horse until she caught up with him.

Worry tightened his gut. "You okay?"

She pulled a face and said, "I think I have saddle sores."

Jag cringed. He could relate. "I think maybe we overdid the riding on your first few days here." He tapped his lap. "Maybe you'd like to hop on over here and ride bareback with me."

Heat moved into her cheeks, and as she tucked her hair behind her ear, she gave him a sensuous, naughty look before saying, "Maybe later."

"Maybe? Hell, cowgirl. There's no *maybe* about it," he said, his voice dripping with promise. "I'm going to hog-tie you and have my way with you all night long."

"Jag," she said, the want in her eyes exciting him as one of the guests rode past, easily able to hear what he was saying.

Jag grinned and kicked his heels in, taking the lead as

they made their way back to the lodge. His cock ached as he thought about what he had planned for Alix tonight, and he picked up the pace, happy the adventure was over, because he couldn't wait to get started.

After returning all the horses, the sun began setting in the west, and he felt his stomach grumble. But his hunger could wait. He was starving for more than food at the moment.

Tired, the guests filed out of the barn, headed toward the lodge for dinner. All alone inside the stable, he stepped up behind Alix, who was running her hands over her horse. His dick twitched as he watched her, wanting that kind of attention on his body, one part in particular.

"Hey, beautiful," he murmured in her ear, and loved the way she relaxed into him. "My place or yours?"

"Aren't you original," she whispered, turning to face him, her hair a tangled mess, her cheeks pink from the afternoon sun. His heart missed a beat. She'd never looked sexier.

He slid his hands around her waist and down her back until he reached her ass. "About these saddle sores," he said.

She arched a brow. "What about them?"

He dipped his head. "If you'd like, I could kiss them better."

Her eyes lit with desire, and as her mouth curved sensuously, a bell sounded outside. "I think that's our dinner bell."

"We'll order in, because right now, baby, there's only one thing I'm interested in putting in my mouth." A small sound caught in her throat as he grabbed her hand and tugged. "Come on."

Strides determined, he led her to his room in the lodge. Once inside, he peeled his sweaty shirt off. She stood there staring at his body as he walked up to her and slowly started unbuttoning her blouse.

"How about you join me in the shower?"

She nodded as he pushed her shirt off her shoulders, letting it fall to the floor. His hands went to her bra. "You have the most beautiful body. I think I want you naked for the rest of the week."

"I don't think the other guests would appreciate me walking around the ranch naked."

He arched a playful brow. "Who said anything about leaving this room?"

She looked at the bed. "I think I'd like to disappear inside this room with you for the rest of the week."

Jag grinned and led her to the bathroom. He turned on the water, and they both finished undressing. He climbed in and pulled her in with him, letting the water wash the day from their skin. He soaped his hands and rubbed them over her body, paying extra attention to her nipples and the sweet juncture between her legs. She moaned and widened for him, but he wasn't going to give her what she wanted. Not yet.

Once thoroughly cleaned, she turned the soap on him and spent a long time lathering his throbbing erection.

She licked her lips, and he throbbed in her hands. He growled and pulled away before he shot off right then and there.

She pouted. "Hey, I wasn't finished."

"Yeah, but I nearly was," he said, and grabbed two towels from the rack. He tied one around his waist and wrapped her in the other one, then, catching her off guard, he tossed her over his shoulder. She yelped, but he ignored her cries and carried her to the other room where he dropped her on the bed.

Her hair flared around his pillowcase, and he just stood there, taking his time to look at the beautiful, smiling woman sprawled across his bedding. She was so perfect. And he was so fucking lost—in her.

"Alix," he murmured.

"Jag," she said, and crooked her finger, urging him close. As his erection tented the towel, she dropped her gaze and said, "Didn't you say something about a surprise?"

With his hard-on thickening, aching to be inside her, today, tomorrow, forever, he walked over to his video equipment and pressed a button. When he turned back to face Alix and saw passion moving into her eyes as she zeroed in on the action taking place on the TV screen, he knew this was one surprise she really liked.

Chapter Five

"Jag," she whispered, her glance going from the television screen to the gorgeous, half-naked man standing close and back to the television again. She looked at the woman on the screen and hardly recognized herself. Desire thrummed through her veins, and she realized that even though he'd been letting her call the shots, he was the man in control, the man guiding her and freeing her sexually.

"How...when?" she asked, even though she already knew the answer to that question as she watched Jag lavish her body with attention on the television, her soft moans of pleasure filling the room through the speaker.

"I left the camera running. I thought you might enjoy a playback."

Seduced by the scene unfolding before her, a tremble moved through her body as she watched the action from the other night. She was shocked, even though she shouldn't be. Jag knew so much about her. More than she knew about herself, actually.

She swallowed, her hands going to her breasts in much the

same way as they'd done in the clearing, feeling completely at ease touching herself with Jag watching. Jag's growl simply prompted her on, and she pinched her nipples hard before rolling them between her fingers. An erotic whimper bubbled in her throat, heat settling deep in her womb.

He dropped his towel and stepped up to the side of the bed. Her mouth watered when she caught sight of his big, beautiful cock, so hard and ready for her. Sexual energy swamped them, and she could feel his desires and needs, knew they matched her own. She breathed in his clean, soapy scent, and sensual overload nearly fried her brain as her gaze swept the length of his solid body.

"You are so sexy," he murmured, and just as he was about to crawl over her, she threw her legs over the mattress, aligning her mouth with his swollen crown.

He gave her a perplexed look and ran his hands along her neck. "What are you doing?"

"Something I've wanted to do for a while now," she managed around a lump forming in her throat.

She closed her hands over his girth. He was hard and swollen, and she could feel the tension in him as she reveled in the thickness and texture. He growled when she wet her lips, leaned forward, and flicked her tongue over his crown, tasting the tangy juice pooling on his tip.

"Mmmm," she murmured, loving the way he pulsed in her hands, the way his magnificent body rippled from her touch.

His deep tenor seeped under her skin. "Jesus Christ, Alix."

Her pussy throbbed, and lust sang through her blood from the excitement of knowing she could rattle him. "Do you like this?" she teased, running her tongue along his length as she cupped his balls with exquisite gentleness.

She glanced up the length of his body, and his eyes shimmered with heat as he watched her mouth work.

Drowning in sensations she'd never felt before, she dragged her tongue over him, a slow, lazy caress that had him cursing under his breath. It secretly thrilled her to know she could do this to him, and made her feel bolder than ever before. Her heart thudded, full and happy. This man had awakened something in her, freed her in a way no one had ever done before.

A sound caught in her throat and Jag palmed her face. "Alix?" he asked.

With her emotions on a roller-coaster ride, she lowered her head and took his cock into her mouth. He gently fisted her hair as she moved her head, taking him as deeply as possible.

"That's so good," he said, his voice hoarse and deep. Pleasure resonated through her as she fucked him with her mouth. His hips rocked, his hands tugged her hair, and her insides soared. It just didn't get any better than this. After this week, how she could go on without him was beyond her.

She licked and sucked, wanting him to let go so she could drink him in, but he had other plans. Full of blood, his cock throbbed, his veins swelling and pulsing as his orgasm mounted. He gripped her shoulders, his fingers burning on her skin, sheer agony etched on his face as he eased her off him.

"Jag," she complained, but her cries of protest were lost on a moan when he pushed her back, dropped to his knees, and buried his face between her legs.

"Yes," she murmured, spreading her arms wide across the soft blankets. He swiped his tongue over her sex, and she nearly came unglued with that first sweet lick. His tongue circled her swollen bud, and he put a thick finger inside her. With every erotic stroke, stimulating her nerve endings, he feasted on her. Honestly, the man was just too good to be true.

She pitched her hips forward and writhed under his care.

As warmth seeped into her soul, blistering heat exploded inside her, and she nearly sobbed with pleasure. His tongue swirled in a way that drove her wild. Her body spasmed as he fueled the flames. But before he allowed her to tumble over the edge, he climbed over her, dragging her to the center of the bed.

"I need to be inside you, sweetheart," he said, the longing in his voice stirring her emotions as his warm breath teased her flesh. "I want us to come together."

He lowered his head, and the look on his face was pure ecstasy as he kissed her with such passion and emotion it left her gulping for her next breath. Their tongues tangled, and she reveled in the taste of herself on his lips.

She tugged him to her, his body pinning hers to the bed, as he gripped her legs to widen them.

"I need you to take me deep. Can you do that?"

"Yes," she cried out, and curled her legs around his back, granting him better access as her body ached for so much more from him.

He plunged into her, and they both cried out. She threaded her fingers through his hair and moved her hips, welcoming every inch of him into her body. Pressure brewed in the depth of her womb as he pumped harder, like he couldn't get close enough, deep enough.

She arched into him, and Jag put his mouth over hers, swallowing her soft cries. The television continued to play in the background, but as her sex muscles gripped him hard, her thoughts scattered, unable to focus on anything but this man and what he was doing to her.

A storm moved through her when he slipped a hand between their bodies to touch her clit. Her body vibrated. Violently. The man had a talent for knowing just what she needed.

Heat swirled around them, racing over her body and

exploding her senses. She raked her nails over his back and skimmed his sinewy muscles, enjoying the feel of his sculpted body as he moved urgently over her.

"You feel so good," he murmured as he bent to take one of her nipples into his mouth. He laved her gently and then bit down. Teetering on the edge of ecstasy, she cried out, her body becoming pliable in his arms.

Lost in the sensations, she liquefied under his touch, and then suddenly the pressure building in her body became too much to bear.

Her sex fluttered, every nerve in her body alive and on fire. "Jag," she said, "I'm so close."

His body broke out in a sweat, and he threw his head back, urgent need coloring his voice when he said, "Me, too, baby. I'm there. Come with me."

She held him tighter, crushing her breasts to his chest as she let go, her pussy clenching hard around his cock.

"Oh, fuck," he growled, and a heartbeat later, a rush of air exploded from his lungs as he gave himself over to the pleasure. She felt him release inside her, his cock throbbing and swelling, his seed filling her body with warmth.

Barely able to breathe as they rode out the waves together, she panted, gasping for air, but still couldn't seem to fill her lungs. They held each other tight for a long time, and eventually, the world around her finally started coming back into view. She ran her hands through Jag's hair, the intensity of their sex stealing the air from her lungs and seizing her muscles.

"So good," she murmured as his muscled bunched. "So damn good."

He lifted his head and smiled. It was filled with such tenderness that her throat clogged as her insides wobbled. "Not good, sweetheart," he said, teasing. "Perfect." He released a sigh, the soft cadence in his tone warming her from head to toe.

She drew his head to her chest, holding him to her heart as he fell over her. Basking in contentment, she soaked in his warmth. She touched his face, rattled by the things he made her feel, the things he did for her. She squeezed her muscles, holding him inside her body, never wanting this moment to end. She was falling, drowning in sensations, in need—for Jag—and was helpless to stop it. How could she ever go back to being dutiful, straitlaced Alix after a week in Jag's bed?

She wasn't the same woman anymore.

Chapter Six

As her glorious, fun-filled, sexy time with Jag came to a close, Alix woke to the sounds of birds chirping and turned to look at the man asleep beside her. Her heart thumped. It had been almost one week since she'd first stepped foot on the ranch. For the most part, Alix had been able to shelve her concerns about her fiancé and future, deciding to simply enjoy Jag and a week of sex.

But as the week came to an end, she was in trouble. She'd allowed herself to feel too much and had fallen hard for him. He might have asked for sex, but he'd pushed her to open up, to become the woman she was meant to be, and it left her wanting more. It wasn't just their time in the bedroom that drew her in. She loved talking to him, and he listened, really listened, when she bared her soul. Telling him about Nelson had been easier than she thought. He didn't pity her. No, he wouldn't waste his time on pity. Instead, he helped her discover what *she* really wanted. And what she wanted was him.

But even if he did want a future with her, she wasn't

the girl for him, and it wasn't just because they came from different worlds. Her hand touched her stomach. Jag deserved to live in that big old house—with a family—and she couldn't give him that. The last thing she wanted was for him to end up cheating on her with someone who could give him what he wanted.

That stopped her. Jag was a good man. The best one she knew, and he'd never cheat, but that didn't mean he wouldn't grow to resent her. She couldn't do that to him, or to herself.

No, she needed to step away, give him the space and freedom to find the woman who could give him everything he wanted and deserved to have.

Raw emotions squeezing her heart and tears pricking her eyes, she tiptoed through the room until she found her clothes. She pulled them on quickly, and quietly made her way back to her room. It was time to pack up, get on the plane, and get back to the real world. She could barely breathe as she hurried down the hall, but she spun around when she heard a loud sound at the foot of the stairs. A pair of dark angry eyes met hers, and her heart lurched, the bottom falling out of her world.

Jag stretched out on the bed, and with no hurry to do anything but wake up and make love to the woman who had given herself to him over and over again, in so many ways, he lay there, basking in contentment. Birds chirped outside, and a feeling of peacefulness fell over him, because now that he had Alix back in his life, he knew he wanted to make some changes, and the first thing he wanted to do was ask her to move into the big old homestead with him.

He stretched a little farther, and when he found the other side of the bed both empty and cold, he peeled one lid open.

He rolled to his side, but still couldn't find her.

"Alix." He rubbed the sleep from his eyes as he peered into the bathroom. An uneasy feeling moved through him, and his gut clenched. Where the hell was she?

Jag threw his legs over the side of the bed and pulled on his jeans. He hurried to the bathroom. When he found it empty, he made for the door. Yanking it open, he looked up and down the hall. No Alix.

Shit.

A few fast steps took him to her room, and it was only sheer strength of will that stopped him from tearing the door clear off its hinges.

Despite the storm going on inside him, he knocked softly. "Alix," he whispered, "Are you in there?" When he met with no answer, he tried the knob to find it locked. Why the fuck was she locking him out? Frustration boiled his blood. Something was wrong, very wrong, but did it give him the right to pound down her door? No, it didn't.

He ran his hands through his hair and knocked again. This time he heard a soft cry coming from the other side.

Alix!

He drew a quick breath and kicked the door. It flung open and smashed against the wall, the sound reverberating down the quiet hall. He heard a gasp, and a familiar heaviness pressed against his heart as he looked at the woman he loved…in another man's arms.

Un-fucking-real.

"Jag," Alix squeaked out. He turned to her, and conflicting emotions passed over her eyes when they met his. The pale, stricken look on her face haunted him. Had she grown tired of slumming with the boy from the wrong side of the tracks and invited her fiancé to the ranch to collect her? Was she planning to go back with him, to fall back into the life laid out for her?

"Get the fuck out of here," the guy said to him as he hauled Alix closer, his hands tugging at her in a possessive way that filled Jag with rage. "Or I'll put you out of here."

He clenched down on his jaw, his stomach roiling. He laughed harshly even though this wasn't funny. Despite the man's warning, he took a step closer. He spotted her suitcase on the bed, her clothes tossed inside. He looked back to the man clutching Alix like he was afraid she was going to flee and shook his head.

Son of a bitch.

"Take your fucking hands off her," Jag said. "Or I'll take them off for you."

"I'm her fiancé, and I'm here to take her back home where she belongs. She made a mistake coming here, and she knows it."

Jag angled his head. "Do you have a hearing problem?" he asked, giving him one last chance to get the fuck out of there before he personally threw him out.

"Jag," Alix said, her voice pleading, like she was trying to make him understand.

He scoffed and without taking his eyes off Nelson, he said, "So this is the asshole who cheated on you, got another woman pregnant, and still expects you to stand behind him."

Alix opened her mouth to answer, but her fiancé cut her off. "The name is Nelson, and Alix and I have worked it all out. Now if you'll get out of the way."

"Really? Because the Alix I know wouldn't stand for your slimy shit."

Alix pulled out of Nelson's grasp and squared her shoulder. "That's right," she said. "And my only mistake was getting involved with you in the first place."

That's my girl.

Nelson reached for her again and dragged her against him. Standing as still as a stealth soldier, Jag sized the man up.

Nelson was a big man; the fight would be fair.

She struggled against him, but this time his grip was too tight.

"Get your hands off her," Jag said.

"It's okay, Jag," she said, sounding breathless. "I can handle this."

"I know you can. But he's touching you, and he shouldn't be. Do you want him here?"

Alix looked from the man holding her to Jag. And then she shook her head. That was all he needed.

Jag stormed across the room, hauled the guy off her, and shoved him toward the door.

"You had your chance, pal. This is my ranch, and you're trespassing. We tend to lay down the law when it comes to that sort of thing. And when it comes to manhandling a woman— especially mine—you'll be lucky if you'll be able to walk out of here by the time I'm done with you."

Nelson stumbled and then climbed to his feet. He charged. But Jag drew back and punched him square between the eyes, knocking him to the floor.

Nelson groaned and clutched his forehead. "You're going to pay for this," Nelson sputtered.

"Yeah, feel free to send the bill," Jag said.

"Alix, your mother has been worried sick about you. When she hears about this, about him," he seethed as he shot Jag a warning glare, "you'll have some explaining to do."

Jag grabbed Nelson by the scruff of the neck and lifted him to his feet. "Alix doesn't have to explain herself to anyone, least of all you." He tossed him out the door and said, "The plane will be here at one sharp. Be on it, and don't let me see your face until then."

Jag slammed the door and turned to face Alix, who stood there, her arms hugging herself as she stared at him.

"He found the invitation," she answered.

His features softened when he looked at her. "I figured it had to be something like that."

"He wanted—"

Jag lowered his voice. "It doesn't matter what he wanted, Alix. What matters is what you want."

She went quiet for a moment and then whispered, "Thank you."

Jag stepped up to her and brushed his thumb over her cheek. A riot of emotions erupted inside him when he saw the warmth in her eyes. "For what?"

She swallowed and waved her hand around the room. "For seeing this for what it really was. With your job, I was sure you would logically jump to the conclusion that I'd run back into Nelson's arms when you saw him here with me. I'd never want you to think that I'd do something like that."

He dipped his head. "Alix, I know who you are, and you wouldn't do that."

She blinked up at him. "So you never thought it? Not even for a second?"

He grinned. "Okay, well, maybe for a second, but hey, cut me some slack, I was half asleep."

She exhaled slowly. "I'm sorry he came here and you had to deal with him."

"I'm not."

Her eyes widened in surprise. "You're not?"

"Nope, I've been itching to beat the shit out of him for quite some time now." Alix laughed, and he pulled her closer. "Are you okay?"

"I will be."

He looked at the suitcase, and a heaviness fell over him. "You were packing anyway, weren't you? You were leaving."

She pushed away, and when she turned from him, it felt like a slap to the face, or worse, a knife slicing through his heart.

"I have to go," she said quietly.

"Just to deal with things back home though, right?" His heart pounded, and a big fucking knot tightened his stomach. "You are planning on coming back, aren't you?"

"No, Jag," she said, her voice cracking. "I won't be back."

Jag clenched down hard enough to grind bone and spun her around to face him. He spotted tears in her eyes. "I thought we had something special. I thought you cared about me, about us."

She tried to look away, but he wouldn't let her. "I do, which is why I have to go."

He raked his hands though his hair and frowned in confusion. "Alix, you're not making any sense."

She stepped away and walked to her window. He traced her steps and followed her gaze. Off in the distance sat the old homestead, one he wanted to share with her.

"You've given me everything this week," she said, her voice bleak, sad. "You've taught me so much about myself, and I want to give you everything, too. The only way I can do that is by leaving."

Her hand crept to her stomach. What the fuck? She was leaving because she couldn't give him kids? Like hell he was going to let her do this. He grabbed her by the shoulders and walked her to the bed. When she sat, he knelt down in front of her. "Alix, sweetheart. I'm in love with you, and if you can't conceive, then we'll find another way to fill our home with kids."

Her glance went to the door. "But Nelson…"

"I'm not that guy." Tension tightened his muscles. "I'm not anything like him."

"No, you're not. You're the best man I know."

"I'd never do to you what he did."

"I do know that, but what if you grow to resent me? You told me your father grew to resent your mother when she got pregnant, and he couldn't go off to college on his scholarship because he had a family to take care of."

"I'm not my father, either."

When she lifted her gaze, stared into his eyes, he stood and held his arms out, baring himself to her. "I'm just a man, Alix, who's in love with you and will do anything in the world to make you happy."

She sat there staring at him for a long time, and his heart beat faster. Christ, he loved that she cared enough to walk away, but the life he wanted was with her. She had to see that.

"Alix," he said, waiting for her to say something. "Talk to me."

She stood and shifted. His heart sank. She was leaving him. But then she held her arms out and said, "And I'm just a girl, Jag. A girl who wants to be loved by you and will do anything in the world to make you happy."

His heart soared as he pulled her into his arms, lifting her clear off her feet. "If you want to make me happy, then get naked and get on that bed."

"Jag," she said breathless, looking at the door he'd tossed her ex out. "Shouldn't we take care of business?"

"I am taking care of business. The doctor said there is a chance you can get pregnant, right?"

"Yeah, a small one."

"Then I think we should still practice."

She squealed as he tore open her blouse, her buttons clattering to the floor as he tossed her on the bed.

"What do you think it will take?" she asked playfully.

He ripped off his pants, his cock throbbing to be inside her. "Hours of *hard* work. Days. Months even."

"Months?"

He climbed over her and smoothed her hair off her face. "Years, even."

She wet her lips, and he saw love reflecting in her eyes.

"Years, you say."

"Maybe even decades. Whatever it takes to make it happen."

"You do seem to be good at making things happen."

He grinned as warmth, love, and trust leaped between them. "I'm good at a lot of things."

Her arms snaked around his neck. "Jag," she whispered into his mouth as she widened her legs to him, giving him both her heart and body. "Stop talking and show me."

His lips found hers as he pushed high inside her. They held each other tight, and while neither knew what the future held for them, as long as she was in his life, and in his bed, it was going to be one hell of a sweet ride.

Epilogue

One year later

Down on her hands and knees, Alix picked the last yellow bean from her little garden and put it in the straw basket beside her. She was about to turn her attention to the ripe cherry tomatoes, perfect for tonight's barbecue with their friends, when a shadow fell over her, blocking the late-afternoon sun from her body and her plants.

"Hey, beautiful."

Her heart missed a beat as she looked up to find Jag smiling at her. She glanced at his outstretched hand and placed hers in it. A little tug brought her to her feet, and when his gaze roamed over her face, a deep concern in his eyes, she went up on her tiptoes and planted a warm kiss on his mouth. God, she loved him so much.

"You look flushed." He placed a palm on her cheek, his eyes narrowing. "I think you've been in the sun too long."

She laughed. "I'm fine," she assured him. Honest to God, these days he was like a mother hen. But she secretly liked all his attention, no matter how much she protested. His brow furrowed as his hand went to her belly. She shook her head and closed her hand over his. "*We're* fine."

"I have to take care of my girls," he said, dropping to his knees to press a kiss to her bulging tummy. True to his word, he had made love to her nearly every day until she got pregnant. She hadn't expected it to happen so fast, or at all, but was chalking it up to a miracle. She'd been taking it slow, careful, but the doctors said everything was looking good as she entered her third trimester.

Her stomach took that moment to rumble, and they both laughed. "She's an eating machine," Alix said.

"I have six steaks marinating, but maybe I should have put an extra one on for her." He glanced at his watch, then grabbed her basket. His arm slid around her body, and he splayed his fingers over the small of her back in that possessive little way that always made her heart catch. "Come on. Let's get you out of the sun."

"I just want to grab some tomatoes."

"Let me."

Her hair fell down her back as she tilted her face to catch the last of the afternoon rays as Jag bent, plucked a few tomatoes, and placed them in the basket. A moment later, his hand captured hers and they leisurely walked to the front of the beautiful old homestead they'd slowly been making their home.

"Let's sit for a bit," she said, feeling a little winded with all the extra weight she was carrying. "We still have a few minutes before everyone comes."

She climbed the steps, running her hand along the freshly painted handrail, the perfect rail for her daughter to slide down. She breathed in the fresh country air and stole a glance around the ranch. A small breath fluttered past her lips, a bone-deep contentment radiating through her body as she settled on the porch swing Jag had constructed for her. He sat beside her and held her hand, both lost in their own thoughts as they looked out over the sprawling land.

The last year hadn't been all happy times and smooth sailing, but with Jag by her side, helping her deal with Nelson and her parents, it made it that much easier. At first she thought her mother and father were going to disown her, but they were slowly coming around and finally seeing Jag for the man he was. Her mother even talked about visiting and helping her with the baby. She turned, taking in Jag's strong profile. He was such a sweet, caring man with more integrity in his pinkie finger than any of the men from her parents' social circle.

Walking away from politics was the second-best thing she'd ever done. Marrying Jag was the first. Now, instead of running political campaigns, she helped run the kids' courses on the ranch. She touched her stomach. Although this year, with a precious bundle to protect, she was more of a director. Next summer, she hoped to be hands-on. Thanks to Jag, she'd found her voice and her passion. Maybe someday she'd go back to school and earn that education degree she always wanted. Until then, she just wanted to enjoy her pregnancy, and life in the slow lane.

A noise sounded and they both turned to see Coop and Julia exiting the small cottage where Coop's mom lived. Her Alzheimer's was progressively getting worse, but with Julia by his side, it helped Coop cope. She waved to them as they made their way over. She scanned the gorgeous little house high up on the hill that Mac had built for Jess — a place with no internet, no distractions. One hundred percent unplugged. She loved that he had done that for her. She spotted them coming down the hill and waved.

"How about Lindsay?" Jag said, and she turned to him.

For six months now he'd been tossing baby names around,

and it warmed her heart to see him so happy.

She squeezed his hand. "Actually, I've been thinking."

"Yeah?"

"How about Charlotte?"

His mouth fell open, and he blinked, but not before she caught the tear that threatened to fall. "You...you want to name her after my mom?"

She shifted to face him and put her hand on his cheek. "Of course I do. I'm just sorry I never got to meet her."

He cupped her face. "Alix...I...that means so much to me."

"You mean so much to me."

"How did I ever get so lucky?" Soft lips met hers. "I love you, baby."

"I love you, too."

He inched back and winked at her. "Do you think we could cancel the barbecue and head inside so I can show you how much?"

She laughed. His lovemaking had been so gentle and tender since the pregnancy, and while she'd like to take him up on his offer, footsteps on the gravel path heralded their friends' approach.

She gave him another quick kiss. "Nope, but I'll hold you to it tonight."

"Get a room already," Mac teased as he climbed the stairs, his arm around Julia's waist.

They all laughed, and as Jess and Mac joined them, Alix shook her head and looked at the five people she considered her family. She never would have thought that a ridiculous plan to find love—forged by three guys over too many beers—would turn out with three happy endings. She was only glad it had.

Acknowledgments

A huge thank you to my awesome editor, Candace Havens. Your insight is brilliant and you are such a pleasure to work with. I'm looking forward to putting the shine on many more books with you.

About the Author

New York Times and *USA Today* bestselling author Cathryn Fox is a wife, mom, sister, daughter, and friend. She loves dogs, sunny weather, anything chocolate (she never says no to a brownie), pizza, and red wine. Cathryn has two teenagers who keep her busy and a husband who is convinced he can turn her into a mixed martial arts fan. When not writing, Cathryn can be found laughing over lunch with friends, hanging out with her kids, or watching a big action flick with her husband.

Discover the **Playing for Keeps** *series…*

SLOW RIDE

Lately, something hasn't felt right for successful doctor and weekend cowboy Chase Cooper. Damn it, he's *lonely*. With an eye on settling down with a nice girl, Coop invites his high school best friend down to his ranch to see if maybe she's the one for him. Instead, her twin sister shows up. But one glance at hotter-than-sin Coop, and Julia Blair knows her little farce is more like playing a dangerously hot game. Because what this cowboy wants, this cowboy gets…

WILD RIDE

Marketing Tycoon Tyler Mackenzie, a.k.a. Wildman Mac, has a knack for knowing what people want and, more importantly, what they *need*…so when he decides to show sweet and sexy yoga instructor Jess Gray that she's the one for him, he puts a seductive campaign into motion. For good girl Jess this is one week of living out her fantasies, but Mac is determined to make this wild ride last forever.

Also by Cathryn Fox

HOLD ME DOWN HARD

When Eden Carver, Iowa farm girl turned NY actress, decides to seduce the sexy cop next door, she begins to wonder if she's bitten off more than she can chew. The last thing Officer Jay Bennett wants is to cross a line with the sweet and innocent country girl. A naïve girl like Eden doesn't belong in his dangerous world. He knows he needs to walk away from temptation, but when sweet little Eden bites back, it tilts his world on its axis. Because biting back changes everything.